The Ghost Dentist of Inverness

Thomas M. Meine
Catriona MacSwallie

The Ghost Dentist
of Inverness

Bibliographic information published by the
Deutsche Nationalbibliothek:

The Deutsche Nationalbibliothek lists this publication in the
Deutsche Nationalbibliografie; detailed bibliographic data
are available on the Internet at http://dnb.dnb.de

© 2025 Thomas M. Meine & Catriona MacSwallie
Publisher: BoD · Books on Demand GmbH, Überseering 33,
22297 Hamburg, bod@bod.de
Print: Libri Plureos GmbH, Friedensallee 273,
22763 Hamburg

2026 edition

ISBN: 978-3-7557-6137-2

CONTENTS

Page

Tae a Thistle

Tae scots yer Mair than just a flower,
Yer a symbol o' great strength an' power,
Wrapped in shades o' purple an' green
Yer the bonniest flower this land has seen.

Some folks say yer jist a weed,
But we Scots ken yer a mighty breed.
Yer delicate yet strong an' bold,
An' worth mair tae us than silver or gold.

Aye yer loved by Scottish heart's,
An' ye always wur right fae the start,
Wi' yer purple heeds and spiny stems,
Yer the richest 'o all oor Scottish gems.

THE GHOST DENTIST OF INVERNESS

I.

Fiona MacGill, hailing from Drumnadrochit, about 15 miles away from Inverness, is an unusual young lady. She is sweet, fun-loving, and intelligent. Above all, she is incredibly wealthy. While there may be many girls like her, it is not her wealth that makes her stand out. What truly sets Fiona apart is her ability to see ghosts and her fearless attitude towards them.

She is not blonde, as the Gaelic language implies (fionn – fair, pale), but has long reddish hair. She could not have inherited this hair color from either her mother or her father. Strangely, there was also no trace of reddish hair in either of her grandparents' families. It's no wonder that rumours arose suggesting that she was somehow foisted on her parents. Whatever, this is now entirely irrelevant concerning her inheritance rights. Her younger brothers, Archie and Finley, have passed away – or drowned, to be precise – and after her parents' tragic death in a house fire, she became the sole heiress to a sizeable estate and fortune.

Drumnadrochit, situated on the western shore of Loch Ness in the Scottish Highlands, is a charming little town that has become a popular tourist destination, especially since a monster called 'Nessie' occasionally sticks its head out of the pond. Before moving, the MacGill clan had lived for centuries in Dochgarroch at the northern end of Loch Ness, close to Inverness, the capital of the Scottish Highlands, where the water flows into the River Ness, continuing through Inverness and the Moray Firth before eventually reaching the North Sea.

One day, completely out of the blue, her father, Hamish MacGill, voiced his dissatisfaction with the local pub. This surprisingly prompted him – a man who certainly did not shy away from a few drinks in good company – to move away with his wife and child and settle on a magnificent estate a few miles further down the lake. It was indeed a peculiar reaction, leading some people to speculate that this couldn't possibly be the true reason for their move when they arrived in Drumnadrochit with little Fiona.

Several years later, Fiona stood with her brother Archie at the shore of Loch Ness, looking for the monster, as they often did. She had asked him to pick up the heavy picnic basket standing close to the shore and secured it with a firm loop around his wrist so that he wouldn't lose it. After shouting aloud, 'Look, Nessie is coming up!', she gave him a determined kick in the backside, sending him tumbling into the lake. He sank immediately and never reappeared – especially as she had packed bricks instead of sandwiches.

People did not believe the bystander who had allegedly witnessed the scene. Fiona? Never! Besides, everyone knows that Nessie is a plankton eater, and Archie, like his brother Finlay, was an excellent swimmer.

Loch Ness is part of the Caledonian Canal, a man-made as well as natural river-and-lake waterway, with four beautiful lakes along the way: Loch Dochfour, Loch Ness, Loch Oich, and Loch Lochy (Scots refer to all non-flowing bodies of water as a Loch), connecting the North Sea in the east with the Atlantic Ocean on the other side of Scotland – across the Highlands.

The water doesn't stand still or move towards one side, like one would assume in a normal canal. Here it moves in opposite directions (!) Many things are different in Scotland, but make sense upon closer inspection: While elsewhere, people blow directly into a pipe, in Scotland, they first blow into a bag and then squeeze it with their arm to push the air from there into the melody pipes. This creates a much louder sound due to the higher air pressure, a main characteristic of Scottish music.

The watershed lies between Loch Oich, where the water flows towards the North Sea via the last lock at Inverness, and Loch Lochy, where the water runs to the other end of the canal through the lock at Fort William, and from there into the Atlantic. Both ends of the canal are at the same sea level, but the journey through the Highlands involves overcoming differences in altitude. This, together with the opposite flow directions, is only possible thanks to numerous locks and swing bridges along the way.

The project remained a crazy idea, at least from an economic perspective. For some masochistic boat tourists who find pleasure in getting tortured along that waterway, it is the greatest in the world. Over a length of 60 miles, they find plenty of punitive instruments, like 11 swing bridges and 29 single- or multi-stage locks, amongst which the 8-stage (!!) lock at Banvie, reverently referred to as Neptune's staircase, where it takes 90 minutes to advance a short distance. No wonder that you can occasionally see signs 'for immediate sale', put up by annoyed shipowners hoping to find impulsive buyers for their barge along the shore before they run away.

Loch Ness has no significant surface current, so anything not floating should sink straight to the bottom. However, there are strong, slow-moving, large wave patterns below. Drowned Archie should have been caught in these and ultimately gotten stuck at the last lock outward at Dochgarroch, but Fiona was aware of that. She knows a few things about bathymetry, the study of beds of water bodies. The maximum depth of Loch Ness is often a topic of discussion. Some say it is 750 feet, others speak of almost 900 feet. Since there are numerous caves at the bottom, accurate measurements are problematic. The sidewalls run down abruptly and steeply in some spots, corresponding to a 75° angle on a sloping hillside; hence, the best conditions for sinking the weights-laden Archie.

A year later, it was time to deal with the other brother, Finnlay. She lured him away from the ruins of Urquhart Castle, a popular Nessie lookout and tourist destination just a short walk from her home, to carry out her plans in a more conventional manner, and away from any curious onlookers.

She told him about a leather bag filled with 'sword and sceptre pieces', old Scottish gold coins, she had found in a crevice near the shore, too heavy for her to carry home alone. While he knelt, greedily examining the bag, she calmly knocked him out with a club, tied the bag to his feet, which was not filled with gold coins but a heavy stone, and sank him in the Loch. After all, it would have been a shame to lose another lovely picnic basket ...

Back to the ghosts: The ghost of Canterville, well known from Oscar Wilde's book and various Hollywood film adaptations, had at long last been laid to rest after being condemned for centuries to haunt the living. However, he has recently started haunting again. Fiona was aware of this from several personal acquaintances. She confided in close friends that she had never made a 'big deal' out of it, as she feared it would only disappoint those who strongly believed in Sir Simon de Canterville's ultimate redemption.

In contrast to her reticence regarding Sir Simon, she is quite open and talkative when sharing her other encounters with ghosts amongst a cheerful audience. Her gruesome tales display a blatant lack of respect for spectres and the undead, bordering on pure impudence. She recounts how she once mockingly approached the 'Man Without a Head' and asked him why he never wore a hat. Before the baffled ghost could catch his breath to respond, she laughed and exclaimed, 'Because you don't have a head to put it on, you nitwit!'

Fiona advises ghosts that wander around as mere skeletons to make nightly visits to the used clothing collection.

She even goes so far as to tease bottle spirits, telling them to find a decent dwelling while they can still get their deposit back on their old shelter.

During her time at St Leonards College in St Andrews, she once left an open bottle of Chanel No. 5 in the cathedral crypt and commented aloud, »That's because you never air this place, you stinkers!«

It's therefore no surprise that ghosts flee at her presence. Some even begin to panic or collapse, often leaving behind a lasting and unpleasant stain.

II.

One day, Fiona experienced a severe toothache, and the best place to seek help was the nearby city of Inverness.

The following day, she boarded the bus at the station near the local post office. The short ride took her along the shores of Loch Ness, passing Abriachan and Lochend – the latter meaning 'the end of the loch' (in this case Loch Ness), before continuing to Dochgarroch, with the last Loch towards the North Sea. From there, the road leads via Craig Dunan straight through 'Inverness Leisure' with the 'Kings Golf Club' into Inverness.

At the other end of Loch Ness lies the tiny village of Fort Augustus. Its name derives from the local fortress, named after William Augustus, the Duke of Cumberland. Because of his cruelties, he is also known as 'the Butcher of Culloden'.

For a long time, the fortress served as a Benedictine monastery, and a five-step lock can be found nearby. They could also have called this place 'Lochend', but the name already exists correctly on the other side. 'Everything has an end, just the sausage has two', but Loch Ness is not a sausage with two equal ends; it is a lake with water flowing in and out, and the outflow towards the North Sea suitably marks the end.

However, Fiona isn't thinking about any of that right now as she gets off the bus at the Farraline Park station at the end of Margaret Street in Inverness.

At first, she walked through the streets, feeling quite confused. She rarely runs errands herself and visits Inverness less and less. This has worsened her knowledge of the area and also weakened her sense of direction. It had also been a long time since her last visit to the dentist, and the people she asked for directions were no help.

But then Fiona discovered a nice pub. Like her late father, she doesn't say no to a glass now and then (actually even more often), and went inside to take a break ...

III.

... after a while, she continued her search.

As she walked around, she found herself, as if by magic, in a rundown neighbourhood she had never seen before, and after a while, she came to a dilapidated house, surrounded by unoccupied buildings.

There was a sign on the wall that read 'Dental Surgery' – not 'Dentist' or 'Dental Practice', but 'Dental Surgery'. Strange, she thought.

Perhaps this isn't the right place to go, thought Fiona. In her case, it should only be a minor issue, a little caries – the Latin word for 'decay'.

The Romans also used the term to describe the taste of stale wine. She thought of her wine cellar, which was filled with bottles of the finest quality, although she always preferred a glass of whisky – first in secret and then, after her parents' death, comfortably in the drawing room. She remembered the polyphenols found in red wine that prevent tooth decay. These inhibit the growth of bacterial flora, resulting in healthier teeth, less tartar, and a lower tendency for bacterial proliferation. But a whisky is a whisky ...

A considerable stock of wine survived the fire at her parents' house, as the basement remained intact after the burning candle slipped from her hand, of all places, in front of her parents' bedroom.

The elderly servant, whom she had sent to Edinburgh on the day of the fire to run a few errands, stayed with her after the disaster. His regular 'checks' of the wine cellar steadily reduced the supply, which perhaps explains why he so seldom visited the dentist and didn't know offhand where she could find one.

Yet all her knowledge of Latin and other wisdom was now useless to her, offering no distraction; she urgently needed dental treatment. Despite all her concerns and the house's rather odd exterior, she went in through the front door.

Everything was dark and musty, but as she climbed the stairs, the place appeared clean and tidy, just as you would expect from a doctor's office.

The waiting room contained plain chairs and a table with a few glasses on it. Several bottles were lined up on a shelf on the wall. In the dim light, she could not see what was inside, so she went closer.

As she approached, she saw that the bottles contained an assortment of the finest whiskies. A sip or two now would definitely do her good, she thought, although it would not be good behaviour for a young lady to help herself without asking, but she couldn't resist ...

There was apparently no one else in the practice, so she announced her presence by shouting a loud 'Hello!'

It did not take long before she noticed a flutter in the dim light. Something blue was buzzing around, and strange vibrations filled the room.

'Is there an undead skunk living here?', she thought. 'But no, this could not be! – or could it?'

The blue mist slowly dissipated, revealing a tattered white cloak, at first indistinct and gradually becoming more recognisable.

The next thing to become visible would be a ghost, she figured, as cloth, such as nightgowns or shrouds, is always seen first before the figure emerges. This is due to the typical phantasmagorical-physical sequence of a ghost's materialisation.

Shure enough, an undead skunk, as Fiona liked to call them, appeared, materialising within the white cloth.

It was an utterly ugly, highly unattractive ghost. The decomposing fabric was tightly wrapped around its emaciated skeleton, which was intact only above the waist. Below, everything slithered free. Its face was only a shrouded skull, and its hands hung down with gnarled, claw-like fingers. But none of this struck her as unusual, given what she had already experienced.

Was that really supposed to be the dentist? Anyone else might have fainted, but Fiona just smiled. 'A ghost dentist?' she wondered. Health insurance companies hardly pay for anything anymore, but are they lately deceiving patients here by presenting them with walking holograms, making them believe they are receiving professional dental treatment? No, the dentist seemed genuine, at least for a ghost, though a cleaner and more presentable smock would have been more fitting.

She heard his sonorous voice, inviting her to follow him into the treatment room: *»Thig a-steach«*. This was Gaelic and means 'come in'.

»Right away«, she replied in English, as she wasn't in the mood for chatting in Gaelic.

»Tha mi duilich, dè?« (I'm sorry, what?), came the reply, as if he couldn't understand her English.

To be polite, Fiona answered with *»sa bhad, tha mi a' 'tighinn«*, instead of saying 'I'm coming right away'. Then again, in a louder voice: *»Sa bhad«* – right away.

He had been staring at her the whole time. Finally, he asked in amazement, »You're not a ghost, are you? No, you're definitely not a ghost who comes here as a patient. You are a real, living, beautiful young lady. You shouldn't have been able to see the practice's sign outside or enter the house. You must have special qualities in your blood. How did you manage to get in? Besides, you don't seem scared at all.«

»Me, scared of ghosts? Afraid of the dentist at most«, Fiona replied. She called him *'Fiaclair'* in the Gaelic language, hoping to put him in a friendly mood, but she was completely wrong.

»*Lannsair Fiaclaireachd*«, 'Dental surgeon', he immediately protested: .

Communicating with the ghost proved difficult. Scottish English became standard in the 18th century, but he was much too old to have spoken it. Scots, retaining the structure of British English, has been spoken since the 15th century, and Gaelic, the language spoken when Scotland was founded, has survived to the present day. But from now on, I will spare the reader the constant switching back and forth between languages.

»Dental surgeon? Did they have that kind of job back in those days?«, she asked in amazement. »And anyway, what and where did you study?«

»I was first trained as a barber at the Macleod Barber Shop in Edinburgh«, he explained, »until a customer of noble birth beat me to death and cursed my soul forever for a botched haircut, and I became a ghost. My legs were so tired from standing behind a barber's chair all day that they didn't make it into my ghost form. They're currently stored in a closet in the ghost world.

»Back then, barbers also pulled teeth. We anaesthetised patients with whisky, and in more difficult cases, we hit them with a mallet.«

»By the way«, he continued, »what do you mean by 'back in these days'? How old do you think I am?«

»About 500 years«, Fiona responded quickly.

»That's quite close«, he said, with great astonishment on his face.

»I travelled around a lot at first, haunting here and there. Lastly, I was at Loch Ness until mass tourism arrived in 1933 after someone managed to take a photograph of the monster Nessie, just as it had left its underground caves to peer out above.

»Oh, I'm so glad I'm not around there anymore! Japanese everywhere, baiting the monster with fish and chips. They mess up the shore and attract the rats. When the pests appear, their usual photo frenzy begins.«

»One of them fell over backwards into the pond while taking a selfie with a rat. Fortunately, he made it back to the shore safely, accompanied by enthusiastic hand-clapping and deep bows from his compatriots around him.«

»The Germans come along and give long lectures, categorically denying the existence of Nessie. They claim that a single monster cannot reproduce and will inevitably become extinct. They're such killjoys until we fill 'em up in the pubs. And then, they swear that they saw Elvis with a bagpipe.«

»Oh, yes, and let's not forget the Dutch. They can't do without bikes, not even here on holiday. They storm the Inverness bike rental shop, ignore the left-hand traffic, occupy the best spots for hours, and eat the food they brought with them from home.«

»Well, fed up with this, I remembered my old profession. To bring myself up to date, I spent time at universities, invisibly following dentistry lessons, and learnt a great deal, until I qualified as a dental surgeon.«

»How did you take your exam?«, she asked.

»I followed other exams and guessed the answers to the questions, just like people who watch quiz shows on TV, until I reached a sufficient level.«

»I mostly look after Scottish ghosts now, but I also occasionally receive spectres that come up from England or even from other parts of the world.«

»Say«, he asked again, »don't I scare you at all?«

»Oh my God!« was Fiona's response. »I've seen plenty of ghosts already, and they tend to be afraid of me, not the other way around.«

»By the way«, she added, »what's your name, Mr Dental Surgeon?«

»Armstrong. My name is Armstrong«, he replied. »The Armstrongs are quite a famous clan here in Scotland. Our reputation among the Border Reivers, robber barons and bandits who wreaked havoc in the border region neighbouring England centuries ago, is widely known.'

»Neil Armstrong, the first man on the moon, is one of our descendants«, he went on, »something we are all extremely proud of, despite some people claiming it was all filmed in Hollywood studios.«

»How about checking what's wrong with my teeth first?«, Fiona interjected impatiently.

»I can't examine you, let alone treat you«, the ghost replied. »You are flesh and blood. No, that's not possible – no, not at all.

And how could I settle a bill for that?«, he muttered to himself.

»Come to think of it, how do you account for that in general?« asked Fiona. »Is the 'Ghost Health Insurance' paying for it, perhaps with the gold and jewellery that have disappeared from the castles over the centuries?«

»No, nothing like that. It's done through a bonus system, as with other services provided, such as performing at haunted events or helping out as a water corpse. But you wouldn't understand that anyway«, he went on to say.

»Well, in that case, I'll leave you again«, said Fiona. »Goodbye, Mr Dental Surgeon.«

Armstrong made no effort to respond to her words and merely scowled.

She protested again, at first in a friendly manner and then increasingly petulantly.

The 'dentist', or what was left of him, assumed a rigid posture and remained silent.

»There's a problem«, he finally came out. »I can't just let you go now. You're not getting away from here any time soon. Let's talk it over tomorrow.«

With that, he dissolved and disappeared.

Fiona became painfully aware of her situation. She found herself in an old abandoned house in a rundown, deserted neighbourhood. The street was empty; traffic obviously avoided the area.

She looked out of the window. There was no one around to ask for help. Taking a closer look at her surroundings, she noticed a strange, crumbling ruin close to the house that had once been a watchtower.

IV.

The evening had arrived. She was alone and locked in. The outer doors were firmly secured, and the windows were barred.

She made herself comfortable, treating herself to a glass or two as she waited for things to happen after Armstrong had left – pardon me, dissolved.

Suddenly, Fiona noticed the strange vibrations again. Armstrong was coming back, but instead of a tattered smock, the first thing to appear was a medieval robe.

»This is my domicile«, he said as he stood beside her, pointing to the dilapidated tower outside. »Quite close to the practice«, he added.

He immediately noticed that she was wondering about his clothes. »I'm more comfortable with this, he explained, and besides, I can't treat you anyway.«

»Better than your usual outfit«, she remarked. »The rags you usually wear would be too shabby even for a scarecrow. Couldn't you find something more appropriate to wear as a dentist's smock?«

Fiona looked at him more closely. His former features could only be guessed at, but he was still more or less in one piece, at least the upper part above the empty breeches.

Many haunting ghosts she had come across were in worse condition, especially when their corpses had been quartered or exposed to the ravens.

Despite the insults about his workwear, the ghost bowed politely and complimented the beautiful Fiona. »If I weren't already seventy years old, I could fall in love again right now.«

»Five hundred«, corrected Fiona, paying no further attention to the remark.

»Yes, you're right. Mary Stuart wasn't even born when I was already wielding the razor. Believe it or not, she just made an appointment for tomorrow.«

»Say, were you really able to estimate my age so accurately, or was it just luck?«, he added.

»I have a bit of experience with decaying ghosts – the look, the smell ... «

She noticed the whisky glass in his hand, which he emptied in one gulp. »Well, a Good Evening to you first«, Miss Fiona continued. »Won't you sit down?«

Armstrong nodded his head instead of speaking and emptied another glass that had mysteriously been refilled.

»Thank you«, said Fiona, »please sit down. I need to talk to you seriously.«

»I beg your pardon?«, he replied.

»Please sit down«, Fiona prompted him for the third time.

The ghost floated over to an old-fashioned armchair and lowered himself into it. The situation was rather tense, and they eyed each other without saying a word until Fiona broke the silence: »Do you intend to keep me here forever? It wasn't nice of you to leave me sitting here, locked up, and disappear. Screaming won't help me, as there doesn't seem to be anyone around who can hear me.«

»Since you can't treat me anyway, you should let me go immediately«, Fiona continued. »I won't talk about what I've experienced here, just as I haven't said anything about any other encounters with ghosts«, she lied like a rug. »I have not even mentioned to anyone that the Canterville Ghost still exists – or exists again – if you like.«

»I would be taking too large a risk«, Armstrong replied. »I might stand again in Loch Ness, performing as an interval act between Nessie's appearances amid all those annoying tourists. No, I have not decided what I'm going to do with you yet.«

»I assume«, Fiona went on, »that you would find it difficult to refuse a lady's request.«

»Oh, that would be quite impossible«, the ghost said with old-fashioned gallantry, »especially with a lovely creature like the one we can see here. If I weren't already seventy ...«

»... five hundred«, Fiona interrupted.

»I would do anything«, he added more seriously, coming back to her question. » Anything reasonable, of course.«

Fiona smiled her most convincing smile. »Do I look like someone who would ask for unreasonable things?«, she asked.

»I'm sure nothing you ask for, besides letting you go, could be unreasonable«, the ghost replied with an ingratiating voice, flattering Fiona for a moment. She had the disconcerting feeling that she had lost her composure, for dwelling with a ghost paying her such compliments was almost making her feel like a ghost herself.

But she soon collected herself again. »Well, as I said«, she began. »You can't treat me, and I'm sure there will be more visits from your regular clients in the coming days. I promise again not to talk about what happened here.«

He appeared to be at a loss for words, gulping down two or three more glasses of whisky in quick succession.

»Why«, asked Fiona, »do you always seem to be busy drinking whisky?«

The ghost dentist suddenly looked extremely sad. »I once haunted Lady Nairn's house and fell over drunk. I had a few glasses of red wine too many when I drank to her health. The guests I was supposed to scare to death quickly recovered and just laughed at me. Since then, I've had to drink whenever I'm in the presence of mortals like you. Those are the rules of our ghost association.«

»Are you telling me that you can't just stop it by your own will?«

»Only if *you* wish it, beautiful Miss«, he replied with all his old-fashioned politeness.

»If I weren't already seventy ...«

» ... five hundred«, Fiona interrupted again.

»As for me«, said Fiona, immediately getting back to the point, which seemed to make the ghost very uncomfortable. »What use can I be to you here?«

»Useful for what? Well, as a lady in attendance, perhaps?«, said Armstrong.

»Bah, they don't say that anymore«, protested Fiona. »They are trained professionals nowadays and are called 'dental assistants', although – come to think of it – for a hairdresser, I suppose, calling her a lady in attendance is probably enough ... «

»Dental surgeon«, Armstrong protested again.

»With a self-issued exam«, she said scornfully. »But say«, she pressed him on, putting her logical skills to use she was always so proud of, »you only drink the ghost of whisky, don't you?«

»Certainly, Miss«, the ghost replied. »The bottles in here have remained untouched until you came along, »but it's still as effective for me as it is for you when you drink the real stuff.«

»So, a self-appointed dental surgeon, trained as a barber, drinks the ghost of whisky. Isn't that a bit stupid for you?«

»You'll have to keep up this nonsense as long as I'm around«, she continued, teasing him. »You'll soon have pretty shaky hands – think of your regular customers.«

»I only have to drink as long as you are human«, he replied. »But if you were a ghost, I could stop drinking and hire you as a lady in a ... «

» ... dental assistant«, Fiona corrected him.

»So you're interested?«, said Armstrong.

»For God's sake, no! Let's stop this nonsense«, came Fiona's sharp reply. »You can't turn me into a ghost. I do have the special ability to see ghosts, but as a human being and not as a ghost.«

»All right, I can't turn you into a ghost myself«, he said. »But you could do it. Jump out of the window right here, and I'll send a curse after you ... «

»If they weren't barred«, Fiona said, »I would have jumped out already. I have made little hops like that when I was still a child.«

»And you can't jump after your brothers either«, the ghost said, »unless I let you out. I learnt something from my old contacts in Loch Ness ...«

»All silly rumours«, she abruptly ended the topic.

»The only thing left for you to do is to release me, and for my sake, you can go on boozing«, she went on. »I will find a way out of here somehow, and believe me, I'll stop being cooperative. I'll spill the beans. The superstitious Scots will tear down the house, and I fear, you will find yourself back in Loch Ness as a supporting cast of Nessie.«

»I tell you«, she continued, »there are more and more Chinese coming here. They copy things at home – the castles, the scenery, and Nessie. They might even clone you, too, or take you along right away. The ex-barber, a laughingstock in Shanghai. How would you like that?«

»You don't understand. It's much worse«, said Armstrong. If I quit my job here, I'd only be the drunkard ghost again. They would start gossiping about me again. I'd lose my status, and I would have to scare people in the green light of the second tier of ghostly apparitions.«

»Yes – I have already noticed the different lights – green and blue«, she said. »So the blue one is for the first set of ghosts, and the green one for the second. But I have also seen ghosts without a halo effect.«

He nodded. »It depends on the activity.«

»You'll keep your job as a dentist if you let me go, won't you?«

»Yes, but the risk is too great for me«, said Armstrong. »I'd better have you safe here.«

»And you have to keep drinking«, said Fiona.

»I'm afraid so ... but I could stop, if you want me to – and I would be relieved ... «

»You don't recognise the realities«, said Fiona. »Why shouldn't I want it? I now want it even more now, of course – so keep drinking!«

As she thought of other arguments she could put forward, she noticed that the light around him was still flickering blue. It was a very intense shade of blue, with no hint of green. He obviously (still) held a respected position among his peers, despite everything that had happened, and most likely wanted to keep it. 'Something ought to be made of this ... ', she thought.

The ghost now appeared highly depressed and began to lament.

»To suffer the disapproval of such a charming lady«, said the remains of the old barber, »is such a grievous misfortune that I cannot help reminding you that you are not fully aware of the circumstances in which I live.«

Fiona had to endure his whiny chatter for quite a while before the eternally cursed tooth-pulling haircut spoiler finally departed – or rather dissolved.

When Fiona went to rest, she could not flatter herself into thinking that she had made any particular progress in persuading the ghost to release her.

She noticed that the undead Armstrong's logic was not only strongly influenced by fear of losing his position, but also by the most powerful of masculine characteristics – vanity. This was especially apparent since he had started to consider himself a quasi-Nobel laureate in dentistry.

'I'm afraid it's no use', Fiona sighed to herself. 'And yet he was only a man when he was alive. He can't be much more now that he's a ghost.'

Firm in her belief that a woman's guile will ultimately overcome any man, she poured herself a drink and soon fell asleep.

V.

The following afternoon, Fiona looked sadly out of the window, but her conviction that she would find a solution remained strong.

It was a bright and gentle day. A faint haze shielded the heat, while a southern breeze brought a spicy, refreshing scent.

Suddenly, she heard someone come in through the front door. Despite the darkness, she could make out a person carrying her head under her arm. The face on this head looked very much like that of someone she knew …

… Mary Stuart in one of the many portraits of her.

MARY Queen of *SCOTS.*

Mary Stuart had died on the scaffold a long time ago. It was not surprising that she had come here, of all places. He was probably the only dentist of his kind in the area.

Fiona noted that her severed head was still well preserved. 'After all, she was once a queen and not a barber', Fiona thought, before quietly retreating.

At around the same time, Armstrong appeared, materialising – as usual – after his tattered white smock. He was obviously dressed for work.

When he saw Fiona, he immediately urged her to hide behind a curtain: »I'm going to bring in the patient now. Stay undercover until she leaves«, he said gruffly.

She did not like the way he gave her orders in such an unfriendly, commanding tone. It should have triggered some stubbornness in her, but female intelligence thinks more effectively and more long-term, and she disappeared quickly behind the drapery.

Meanwhile, Mary Stuart took a seat in the waiting room — well, her lower part did, with her head in her lap. Armstrong took it from her, carried it into the treatment room, raised the patient chair as far as it would go, and laid it on top.

The skull was rolling from side to side. He had to work on teeth 6 and 7 on the lower right. With only two hands, he couldn't hold the instruments and the head at the same time, not to mention the fact that he also had to open the mouth, which, in this particular case, couldn't be done by the patient sitting in the next room.

It was Mary Stuart's first visit, and he was not prepared. 'If I only had a lady in a ... I, I mean, a dental assistant', he thought.

»He had no other choice and beckoned Fiona in: »Would you mind giving me a hand – sorry, assisting me – Miss?«

'Should I refuse?', Fiona thought, but being such a nice girl, she gave in and approached carefully from behind, making sure that Mary Stuart's head was not looking in her direction.

Whether it was fate or mere coincidence, the whisky glass had been refilled and was floating towards the dentist. Armstrong took it and emptied it immediately, followed by something he didn't expect: When Mary Stuart's head saw this, vile curses came out of its mouth, followed by remarks about 'lack of professionalism'.

At the same time, the lower part of Mary Stuart, still sitting in the waiting room, rushed in, grabbed her head, and stormed off in a rage. A torrent of swear words echoed through the house. The patient was gone, and Armstrong's reputation was certainly a little more tainted.

Initially, he wanted to chase after her, but he stopped at the last moment, fearing her wrath because Mary has a known reputation for having problems when alcohol is involved in any way.

He knew that Mary Stuart always got upset when she was credited with giving the name to the cocktail called 'Bloody Mary'. This is, at first, a confusion with another Mary, Mary Tudor, Queen of England. She gained this reputation because of her bloody persecution of Christian heretics. But that is also incorrect. In fact, it was a Chicago waitress who had inspired a bartender to come up with this name for this vodka-and-tomato-juice mixture.

Fiona, who had quickly disappeared behind the curtain in time, stuck her head out. She saw that the whisky glass had been refilled. In the distance, the swearing voice of Mary Stuart could still be heard, fading away as she travelled back to her whereabouts.

Now it was clear to Armstrong: he had to send Fiona away and trust her word – or let her become a ghost.

»Truce«, said Armstrong. »Let's be reasonable about the situation until I can come up with a solution.«

»Don't wait too long«, Fiona responded, »it could come to a horrible end for you.«

»I will soon find an answer to all this«, he said.

'Never', thought Fiona. She knew that it was up to her to develop a strategy to get out of this, but what could she do?

Well, at the moment, they had to get along as best they could.

Fiona had finally relented and taken on some helpful tasks and immediately promoted herself. 'Practice manager' was her desired title, which she cheekily asserted. She thought that playing his game for a while would distract him and give her better opportunities to work on her plan.

VI.

The next day, she checked the schedule and saw an entry for a Mr L. Armstrong, arranged for the afternoon. 'Probably one of the ancient members of the clan,' she said to herself.

At 4 o'clock sharp, the patient was coming up the staircase. She couldn't resist taking a quick and sneaky look at him before hiding again. In the dim light, she couldn't get a clear view of his face and could only guess where it must be because he was constantly wiping it with a white handkerchief.

His eyes shone like Meissen porcelain saucers, and under his arm, he carried a polished, gold-coloured object. He seemed to be in a surprisingly good mood. When he opened his mouth, he revealed his dazzling white teeth, with a slight 'trema' [tooth gap] between the upper incisors.

She quickly returned to her hiding place and listened curiously to his voice. She immediately noticed that this was not the Scots way of talking English, nor Oxford-style, nor any other variation from the British Isles. 'If the Armstrongs can fly to the Moon,' she thought, 'they can come from anywhere on this planet'. She was somewhat irritated. But then, when he started singing *What a Wonderful World* in a deep, scratchy voice and played something like a greeting for the dentist on his trumpet, she knew this must be 'Satchmo' [the Satchel Mouth] – Louis Daniel Armstrong.

She was surprised to see him here – as a ghost. Anyway, he could not have been connected to the dentist's Scottish clan.

As with her, some personal details remained unclear. In his case, it was the date of birth. Louis Armstrong had always given the 4th of July, the Independence Day of the United States, as his birthday. This was common among African Americans when they did not know the exact date of birth or the circumstances. But then, once he had become a famous, worldwide celebrated man, they came forward from all corners, also with useful information about his early beginnings, so that one could finally nail down bindingly the 4th of August as his birthday.

Fiona couldn't control herself any longer. She stepped forward and, before the dentist could interfere, she asked Satchmo for an autograph.

Satchmo, not at all surprised by her presence, took a hand off the trumpet and drew something in the air with his forefinger.

Fiona was deeply disappointed. She could not show such an autograph to her friends, written into the air and mirror-inverted from her vantage point.

Many trumpet players are forced to practise outside in the woods due to complaining neighbours. While walking around, they occasionally break an incisor when they run into a tree, but Louis Armstrong cannot run into a tree anymore. He would walk straight through, and besides, he had a problem with one of his molars, not an incisor.

After his tooth had been fixed and he had left, Fiona suggested changing the entry in the book.

»As a practice manager, I'd say we should note his full first name instead of just 'L.'«

Correctness was important to her. After all, she wasn't working in a barbershop – even for short – where people barge in disorderly right off the street.

»Make it L-E-W-I-S if you like«, he said.

Being intelligent and educated, Fiona told him, of course, that down in New Orleans, where Satchmo hailed from, they use the French variant and spell it as 'Louis' and not 'Lewis'.

The dentist did not like this contradiction for the sake of maintaining the hierarchical order:

»Leave the 'L.', I know who he is.«

»By the way«, said Fiona. I would never have guessed that such a nice guy could become a ghost.«

»Well, jazz music isn't everyone's cup of tea«, he said, »and when enough people curse you ... «

»But if so, what about all those bagpipers with their deafening noise?«, Fiona interrupted.

»You don't know everything about ghosts after all«, said Armstrong. You should spend more time outdoors. On certain days, their ghostly shadows march in full regimental strength over Hill and Glen.«

Fiona made another attempt to discuss her release, again without success. 'So be it', she thought, continuing to ponder over her plan. A solution would surely come to her soon. To twist the dentist around her little finger, she mentioned, while sorting through the documents, that he had a few prominent people among his patients. And indeed, that flattered him very much.

He immediately told her about Henry VIII, a patient for whom he had replaced all of his teeth.

»Now, that was a major construction site«, he said, »when Henry VIII's skeleton walked in here. His toothy pegs had almost all fallen out and been lost somewhere. Since he wouldn't wear dentures, I had to implant a lot.«

»You should have also given him a tube of remineralising toothpaste with medical-grade hydroxyapatite to take home«, she wisecracked. »It's the latest thing on the market. Good stuff! Hydroxyapatite is a mineral belonging to the phosphate, arsenate, and vanadate class. It crystallises in the hexagonal crystal system with the chemical composition $Ca5[OH|(PO4)3]$ – if I remember correctly. It's the basis of hard substances such as bones and teeth of all vertebrates.«

»We don't have such a thing in the ghost world«, he replied, sounding astonished. »No chance, you would stay here as a lady in a … I mean as a dental assistant?«

»Practice manager«, she replied. »No, I'm telling you again, loud and clear: Most certainly not.«

Armstrong, somewhat disappointed, went on to talk about his famous client: »At first, his death was kept secret for three days. They wanted to make sure that his son's assumption of power would go through first without any disturbance.«

»As was customary for kings, he was embalmed and transferred to Windsor Castle. Then it was off to the crypt in St George's Chapel. But it was here that the problems truly began: The triumphal arch planned for the crypt could not be completed. They put him into the black marble coffin that he had confiscated during his lifetime from the Catholic Wolsey, Archbishop of York and Cardinal, alongside parts of his crypt furnishings. However, this was just a stopover for him, as his stay in this sarcophagus did not last for long. Things became too expensive and remained fragmented. The cost of the war with France was a major financial burden. There were disputes with a sculptor and repeated interruptions to the work's completion. Then came the sale of various items to raise money, and finally, also the opening of the tomb to make room for the executed King Charles I. During this, a soldier stole one of Henry's bones as a souvenir.«

»The black marble coffin was later used for ...«

» ... the fallen Admiral Nelson«, Fiona interrupted. »He died in the great naval battle of Cape Trafalgar, fighting against the united French and Spanish fleets. This marked the beginning of British rule at sea, and the little Corsican's days were soon also numbered on the continent.«

Quite annoyed by Fiona's cleverness, the ghost continued: »All that was left of Henry was a skeleton, missing a bone, and some parts of his beard on his chin. They left him in this state under a plain stone slab.«

»One can certainly understand that the man at least wanted his teeth to look neat again«, Fiona commented.

The dentist went on: »Some people say that he had all his wives beheaded, but ... «

»I know, I know«, Fiona interrupted again. »That's all nonsense and needs to be put into perspective. Henry VIII was only married six times, and not all of his wives had their heads cut off. In fact, there were only two of them who had suffered this fate. Well, once you have a bad reputation ... «

»One remembers the end of each marriage best with a saying the schoolchildren recite:«

divorced – beheaded – died,
divorced – beheaded – survived

»His last wife, Katherine Parr, survived him by eight years«, she continued, »and was married four times. One of her husbands was the brother of Henry VIII's third wife. Her last husband, a schemer with a greed for power, was beheaded soon after her death.«

Armstrong finally 'had enough', a state that Henry VIII probably also wanted to achieve with his teeth. The dentist said no more about his famous patient, also known as 'England's Nero', but could not resist taking a swipe at Fiona.

»You could have become his seventh wife while he was here. That would have solved the problem of becoming a ghost ... «

»Ghost by a 'divorce'?«, said Fiona. A 'Divorce' would come next in the order, not the scaffold, if you can remember the simple two-line nursery rhyme.«

The ghost gave up and was about to move on to other prominent patients, but Fiona no longer listened. Soon afterwards, he dissolved again.

VII.

Over the past few days, Fiona had searched the entire house from top to bottom in hopes of finding a way to escape, but without success, leaving aside the discovery of a few more bottles of whisky.

She felt increasingly depressed. Unable to find an escape route upstairs through the windows, she went downstairs to the front door again, which was still firmly barred. She carefully examined everything else around – also without any results. 'Another day lost', she thought and angrily stamped her foot, but what was that?

The floor beneath her feet sounded hollow. She pushed an old carpet aside and discovered a trapdoor with a ladder leading down into a dark cellar. Though it was pitch-black, she summoned her courage and began to descend.

There was a greenish light coming from somewhere, like the kind that surrounds less respected ghosts. It allowed her to recognise some outlines, but when her eyes had become accustomed to the darkness, she noticed that she was in a chamber with a corridor leading to another room.

What she saw there sent a chill down her spine. Cowering in a corner was a little boy with a greenish glow around him, staring at her in fright.

It was a ghost, but she had never encountered one so young.

»What are you doing here?«, said Fiona, quite surprised, once she had regained her composure.

»I've been punished for causing the deaths of two people in the fire at a house in Drumnadrochit. I don't know how long I have to stay here.«

»What? You? But that was ... « She quickly swallowed the rest.

»At the moment, I have to prove myself with minor jobs. Today here, tomorrow someplace else. For now, I have to keep pouring whisky for a ghost who runs a dental practice upstairs whenever I'm ordered to. He can't see me – and neither can you – except here in the basement when he's not around.«

»I'll tell you, I have more than enough to do right now. Between my duties as a permanent waiter, I have to stay down here until the end of my assignment. But say, that constant refilling must have something to do with your presence, because I was sent here as soon as you arrived.«

She did not respond to his question, but dared to ask: » Did you really kill two people in a fire in Drumnadrochit?« Her curiosity was too strong for her to hold back.

»Yes, I broke into the MacGill's house at night to steal some silverware. While I was inside, I tripped over a candle that had been lying on the floor. It had already burned out, leaving just a small scorch mark on the carpet.«

'Well,' I thought, 'if I light the candle again, it will burn the rug and a few other things more effectively. Then, amid the general excitement, I will have the chance to grab a few more valuable items.'

»Strange!«, he continued. »Through the window, I could vaguely see a young lady in a nightdress standing outside. She didn't move, and even when the fire spread through the house, she showed no reaction. It was only when the flames were already coming out of the attic, and all was too late, that she cried out for help.«

»Very strange«, Fiona remarked.

»Yes, very strange«, he echoed.

»I died in the fire myself. I had stared at the girl for too long, wondering all the while why she wasn't screaming. By the time I tried to run away, it was too late.«

»But what are *you* doing here?«, he asked, eyeing her curiously.

»Well, I was looking for a dentist to take care of my toothache, and I got into this. Since then, the fellow has held me captive.«

»Why, of all things, a dentist for ghosts? You're not a ghost, and you're still alive and in good health, as one can clearly see«, said the boy.

»I can't explain that either, except that I run into ghosts quite often«, Fiona replied. »But say, can't you help me out of here?«

»I don't see how«, said the boy. »I can go right through doors and walls, but you would need a key.«

»Too bad«, said Fiona. »I can only hope that you will continue to pour him whisky copiously in time; this gives me a chance to get away.«

»For your sake, I certainly hope so«, said the ghost boy. »I will follow your instructions. That might solve my problem too, at least I could stop with the constant and stressful refilling to keep him drunk during your presence. I could be relieved of such menial tasks, but I have given up hope. I am rightly punished for what I have done, unless the last surviving family member, a certain Fiona MacGill, would forgive me. »'I forgive you, Blake!'«, she would have to say.«

»That should be possible«, Fiona said, without considering the effect of her words.

»Why do you think so?«, the boy asked, somewhat astonished.

Fiona said no more on the subject. She felt that the past had caught up with her. Was it not a coincidence that she was here? The brothers, the fire, an upcoming feeling of guilt ... But what could she do now?

VIII.

The next day, when she saw the dentist again, she could barely keep her temper under control. Her disdain for haunting creatures resurfaced, but she ignored him at first and said nothing.

The ghost appeared as usual, saluted, and took sip after sip from his shadowy whisky glass. He had drunk at least half a dozen glasses of whisky, which were being refilled at increasingly shorter intervals – and she now knew who was doing the refilling.

Finally, she deigned to acknowledge his presence.

»Your drinking is getting worse and worse«, she said gruffly. It's so terrible, but I will not make you stop it. What do you say?«

»Good, now I can answer you«, said the ghost, »for I cannot speak until I have been spoken to in the presence of a human being, or they must at least have screamed or gasped in fear of me«, he added apologetically.

»You know, I must continue to drink until I am asked to do otherwise.«

»There won't be an 'otherwise'. I even urge you to keep drinking«, Fiona replied coldly, turning away from him. »I sincerely hope that all that whisky goes to your head, or whatever is left of it.«

»It certainly does«, replied the ghost in a mournful tone. »And in all my ghostly existence, indeed, even when I was 'only' human, I have never been overcome by alcohol in the presence of a lady, except for that slip at Lady Neirn's. But that was due to the red wine, that French plonk.«

»Plonk?«, she asked. »Well, it seems that Lady Neirn did not have my stock of quality wine at her disposal, and it's only 14 to 15% alcohol, unlike our whisky, which is at least 40%, but if you're not used to it ... «

As she spoke, the dentist continued to gulp down the whisky, all the while being watched curiously by Fiona.

»And come to think of it, mortals seldom get to see a drunken ghost. It would be foolish to miss this opportunity without taking a closer look at this phenomenon.«

»Tell me to go away, dance around, or do anything else«, implored the former barber. »Once you've called it an unmissable opportunity and said that you have to take a closer look at a drunken ghost, I am totally in your hands.«

»Then will you let me go now?«, she asked.

A look of despair shone across the ghost's wrapped and mummified face, and for a few moments, the two stood facing each other in silence while the ghost continued to drink.

Fiona watched Armstrong with an implacable expression, and suddenly made the curious discovery that he appeared to be standing on tiptoe. A moment later, she realised that he had indeed risen. The tips of his tattered cloak were repeatedly lifted off the carpet.

At first, she feared that he was about to float away and escape forever. However, on closer inspection, she realised that he was struggling to resist the tendency to rise into the air. The ghost knew that a dissolution would leave him in the earthly realm. Floating away, on the other hand, would immediately take him back to the ghost world. He was holding up his inexhaustible whisky glass in his bony right hand while clinging to the back of a chair with his left, in an obvious effort to keep himself down.

»You seem to be standing on your toes – sorry, smock tips – «, she remarked. »Are you looking for something?«

»No«, the ghost replied, visibly confused, »it's just the 'levitation' that comes from constant drinking.«

Fiona laughed scornfully. »Do you mean that it's a sign of intoxication if a ghost develops a tendency to rise into the air?«

»In our circles, it is considered more correct to use the term employed by the occultists«, replied the ghostly apparition somewhat sulkily. »We speak of it as 'levitation'.«

»But I don't belong to your circles«, Fiona replied firmly, »nor do I sympathise with the occultists.«

»Another question«, said Fiona. »Has it never occurred to you that, in these advanced times, you – and all ghosts, for that matter – no longer enjoy the same respect in public opinion or even in scientific esteem as you once did? Nowadays, you are merely considered a hallucination, you know, and there is no reason why you should be regarded with anything but contempt because you are nothing more than the result of a bad night's sleep following indigestion or mental exhaustion.«

»But you can see that I'm not a hallucination, can't you?«, said the poor ghost dentist in a shaky voice, obviously discouraged.

»Oh, it's just a sensory illusion«, Fiona replied. Any doctor would tell me that and give me a prescription to stop me from seeing you again.«

»But he can't do that now«, said the ghost. »And besides, you can see that you are securely locked up here. Surely, *this* is not a hallucination?«

»Let's not continue this now«, she said. What I wanted to say was this: »Doesn't it seem to you that this is a good opportunity to improve your reputation by letting me go, regardless of what the arrogant ghost club says? Even your fear that I would talk about my experience here should be reconsidered. Spreading the message seems to be more advantageous than disadvantageous.«

»I would give you my word that I will report the case to the Psychical Research Society – only if you agree, of course – and you will subsequently go down in history with a lasting reputation which the incredulity of time cannot destroy. This would make Oscar Wilde's book about the Ghost of Canterville a trashy novel – you, the new Sir Simon de Canterville, with me as Victoria.«

The ghost had meanwhile got into a state of intoxication, which made it extremely difficult for him to resist sailing away through the ceiling, and he clung even more desperately to the back of the chair. »But the Psychical Research Society is not recognised in my circles«, he protested.

»Very well«, exclaimed Fiona angrily, »do what you want! But how will it affect your reputation if your condition worsens, and you are flying back to your circles? In this society, you think so highly of, floating around drunk in the presence of mortals will certainly not earn you respect!«

»Oh, just thinking about it makes me panic!«, wailed the dentist ghost, followed by a cry that made even Miss Fiona's blood run cold. »What a shame that would be!«

»I will do anything you ask«, he moaned.

Fiona jumped to her feet in sudden excitement.

»Are you saying that you will release me now?«

»The wavering voice of the ghost gave her the impression that he had finally given in. »Yes, but you must guide me«, he said. »I know where the key to the front door is hidden.«

»I don't need it myself«, he went on, »and neither do my patients. We can go right through walls and doors, but I prefer to keep the house permanently locked so that no human creature can accidentally walk in here.

»I still wonder how you got in. You must be a bit of a ghost yourself, at least now and then. When your human side prevails, the door remains locked to you. I almost think they don't want such a bad girl like you in the ghost world, and they still waver back and forth in their opinion.«

»Bullsh..«, said Fiona. I'm still alive, so they have nothing to decide; they can do this when I'm dead.«

»By the way«, he continued, »have you never wanted to know who your birth mother was? I mean, the one with the red hair, which no one else in your family ever had? I was able to get this information.«

Fiona had often asked herself that question, especially whenever rumours about her hair colour came up again. Her parents were very secretive about it, whereas her brothers talked about it too often and too loudly for her liking, until she felt it was unavoidable to give them their last bath in Nessie's tub. The dentist, this creepy bloke, must have made enquiries behind her back.

»She was your father's sweetheart in Dochgarroch«, he went on. »Your stepmother murdered her out of jealousy, but spared your life. They sneaked you into the family before your brothers were born. Your father was a real coward and covered up for her crime.«

»I was going to tell you all that if you had accepted my offer to stay here and work for me. Your mother is said to be descended from the witch Gyre-Carling, and there are rumours that she ... «, he wanted to say more, but was interrupted by Fiona.

»This sounds rather adventurous to me«, said Fiona defensively. »But first, I want the key, then the alleged mother-story.«

»Give me your hand«, the ghost said. »I'll otherwise float to the ceiling if I let go of the chair.«

»My hand? That means I ... No, I don't like your clawed fingers. I also doubt that your filthy, smelly, rotten rags you are wearing will withstand the pulling effect«, Fiona replied. »I have another idea.«

Her words became more impertinent. Now that she would be out here soon anyway and not keep her mouth shut afterwards (which she never intended to do anyway), she could somewhat 'spice up the dialogue, which she would – hopefully soon – reproduce to her friends in a merry circle.

»Here, hold on to this, you undead skunk!«, she said.

She picked up a sickle probe from the dentist's kit, holding it out to the ghost, the right way around, of course – with the pointed part facing the patient.

The ghost hastily grabbed it and let out a scream as the tip dug into his bony finger, but he held on bravely.

'Strange!', she thought, as she guided him through the room while he hovered and wriggled above like an excited, captured parrot. 'When you try to knock them away with a stick, it goes through without resistance, and when you prick them with a sickle probe, they start yelling. The alcohol, perhaps ... '

Fiona was amazed by the power of the elevation pulling on her hand, but she remembered that he had drunk a mammoth amount of whisky.

She followed the whisky glass in his waving hand until they came to another room. There, he directed her to a corner and gave signs that she should lower herself to the floor.

Fiona pulled him down after her, and he directed his gnarled hand to a particular panel in the wainscoting.

»Search here«, he said.

In the excitement of the moment, Fiona let go of the sickle probe. The ghost immediately floated upwards like a balloon released from its moorings as the probe fell to the floor.

»Goodbye«, she just managed to call after him. »Thank you so much, you smelly half-skeleton!«

The ghost had drunk more and in shorter succession than ever before, and like a blurry and dissipating cloud above her head, the intoxicated spectre faded away. He was not leaving in a local dissolution, but catapulted up into the void and back into the ghost world, where scorn and derision awaited him. The terrible, long, and reverberating screams that slowly faded into the distance told her that he had realised the awful truth.

IX.

Fiona immediately set about loosening the panel. Armed with useful items lying around, like sickle probes, impression trays, extracting forceps, excavators, bone files, hand chisels, crown pliers, clamp pliers, and angular scissors, she got to work.

In her overeagerness, she hastily snatched the drill without releasing the detent on the feeding, and the entire dentist's chair fell over.

She was in a trance, exhilarated by her triumph over the stubborn ghost. He would now receive his punishment. Why hadn't he continued working here as a respected dentist? He just had to let her go.

She scratched, hammered, drilled, pulled, pushed, pressed, pried, scraped, poked, and tugged, but the panel didn't budge.

There must be a secret mechanism somewhere, she thought, which he, unfortunately, could no longer show her. But when Fiona tries to get her way, she develops tremendous strength, and finally, the panel came loose. But what was that? She only found the dust from centuries past.

He had tricked her. He probably wanted to tell her that the key had been misplaced, hoping to escape his current predicament and buy time.

When she realised there was no key, she broke down and tears ran down her cheeks.

X.

Fiona cursed the dentist, the foulest of words echoing throughout the house. But cursing him now was of no use; that had already been done by someone else, forever and ever. 'This man thought it was acceptable to cheat on a woman', she thought. 'Is this how the 'old-school' gentlemen we hear so much about behave? He got his just deserts!'

She blamed herself. Why had she let him drink so much? She was responsible for his intoxication leading to his elevation, and she should have held on to him more tightly, but who could have expected such a thing? The ghost was still showing the after-effects of its drunkenness the previous day, and everything else came on top of that.

But now, she needed a drink herself, or two, or three ...

Soon she was chanting one of her favourite songs, *'Donald, Wheres Your Troosers'* (Donald, where are your trousers) at the top of her lungs, filling the house with her raucous singing. It's a mocking tune about men wearing kilts with nothing underneath.

But when she became aware again of her tricky situation, she shouted: »This disgusting fellow tried to lead me astray, but I will find my way out!«

XI.

Once she had calmed down a little, she went downstairs to see the ghost boy, hoping he might provide her with some useful information.

He was still there, probably waiting for new instructions, now that his job at the dentist's office was finished. However, he was unable to help her, so she went right back upstairs and relived the scene in her mind.

»Ah!«, exclaimed Fiona, struck by a sudden inspiration. She could see the picture clearly before her again: While the ghost dentist had given her his instructions, he had adopted a strange posture and tried hard to avoid looking at the corner of the room diagonally opposite the one he had led her to.

She sprang forward to move an old sideboard standing in the way, which proved to be quite heavy. 'How did the fragile ghost get it there?', she thought, but then she remembered that there is even a special kind of them – the ghostly furniture movers.

She pulled and pushed. Inch by inch, the sideboard moved, and she finally managed to get it far enough away from the wall. She immediately examined the panelling and scratched, poked, and hammered again. She worked hard for a while, and the sweat stood on her forehead. Just as she was about to give up, she saw dust coming out of a tiny hole when she kicked against the panel in frustration. She took a disposable needle and poked through the small opening. Immediately, the panel moved and slowly opened on a hidden hinge.

Her eyes shone, and her body trembled. There it was – the key!

Her voice overflowed. »Yes, yes, I've got it!«

Of course, she would have been interested in the full story about her mother, but never mind. She won't investigate in Dochgarroch any further – asking too many questions could stir up trouble and jeopardise her position as sole heir. Besides, she no longer had any desire to sink more people into the Loch.

Completely exhausted, she staggered to the stairwell and went downstairs to the front door. She put in the key and unlocked it. But something held her back.

Should she return and shout the redeeming words down the trapdoor? But then, he would know who she was and could probably guess why she had called for help so late while the fire was raging.

Now that she knew the full story, she felt that most of the guilt had fallen from her; after all, *her* candle had gone out before a fire had killed her parents.

Her stepmother was a murderer, her father a coward who had covered up for her crime, and the jealousy of her brothers, offspring of the two, and their spreading of rumours were good reasons to get them both out of the way.

Her inheritance was something she had to protect. 'It was not personal; it was strictly business', she thought.

In any case, Blake was dead, and she could ensure he returned to the ghost world redeemed.

Once again, she pushed the carpet aside, lifted the trapdoor, and yelled down:

»Are you still there, Blake?«

«Yes«, he came up with a faint voice.

»That's good, because I have something to tell you.«

»What is it?«

»I forgive you, Blake!«

The green glow faded. Strong vibrations shook the house, and suddenly everything was illuminated in a bright blue. Blake had gone back in honour.

XI.

Outside, the city was full of life. People were crossing the streets, and cars were going up and down. Colourful stores displayed their goods in the windows.

It was *the* Inverness she knew. Only one house was not inhabited – the one she had just left. Windows and doors were boarded up, the plaster was crumbling, and the roof had seen better days.

She looked for the 'Dental Surgery' sign on the wall, but there was no sign that said 'Dental Surgery', only one that said 'For Sale' and 'Armstrong Real Estate' written below.

Suddenly, she felt strong hands shaking her rather hard.

»Miss, you can't be lying around here on this park bench! What are you doing here anyway?«

A police officer leaned down and looked even more puzzled when he caught the smell of alcohol on her breath.

»Have you been hanging out in a pub? I can smell the whisky. Why are you behaving like this? »Are you heartbroken because you cried so loudly for Blake, whom you want to forgive?«

»Blake? What Blake? I don't know any Blake; you must have misheard.«

»No, Constable. I was just a little tired from all the walking around and must have fallen asleep here«, she said, smiling at him in a particularly friendly way to better his mood.

Meanwhile, across the street, the door to a pub opened, and a man walked over, quite upset.

He pointed at Fiona: »It's been a problem ever since they allowed women in pubs. We had to install ladies' toilets; the male staff must wear pants and leave the kilt at home because women had been lifting them to see what's underneath. Those who had refused were repeatedly harassed by large groups of drunk women who wanted to find out for themselves if he was a real Scotsman.«

»But this young lady here topped everything we have experienced so far!«

»She had a few glasses too many. She fell asleep and was obviously having nightmares, babbling about ghosts and the ghost of whisky.«

»Halfway awake again, she knocked over chairs, tampered with the wall paneling, and tore out some pieces, whilst her ugly swearwords filled the house.

And when she bawled the song 'Donald Wheres Your Troosers', she got the other girls really going.«

»We finally had enough and took her outside for some fresh air.«

»She pointed to the old house over there«, he continued. »Heavily swaying, she said something about a dentist sign that had been taken down before we put her on this bench.«

»Oh, I see«, said the police officer, »now I understand. Yes, I'm also afraid of the dentist myself and have a glass or two beforehand.«

»By the way, young Lady, I know a good one close by. He's just around the corner ... «

»That's all right«, said Fiona, »I'd better take the bus home. But thank you very much, Constable«, and she staggered away, still a little shaky.